THE PENGUIN POETS

PROMISED LANDS

Peter Sacks was born in South Africa and teaches writing and literature at Johns Hopkins University. He is the author of *The English Elegy: Studies in the Genre from Spenser to Yeats*, which won the Christian Gauss Award, and the poetry collection *In These Mountains*. He is married to the painter Barbara Kassel.

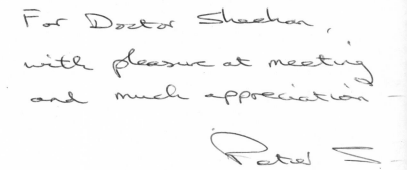

For Doctor Sheehan,
with pleasure at meeting
and much appreciation —

Peter S.

PROMISED
LANDS

PETER SACKS

PENGUIN BOOKS

PENGUIN BOOKS
Published by the Penguin Group
Penguin Books USA Inc.,
375 Hudson Street, New York, New York 10014, U.S.A.
Penguin Books Ltd, 27 Wrights Lane,
London W8 5TZ, England
Penguin Books Australia Ltd, Ringwood,
Victoria, Australia
Penguin Books Canada Ltd, 10 Alcorn Avenue,
Toronto, Ontario, Canada M4V 3B2
Penguin Books (N.Z.) Ltd, 182–190 Wairau Road,
Auckland 10, New Zealand

Penguin Books Ltd, Registered Offices:
Harmondsworth, Middlesex, England

First published in the United States of America by
Viking Penguin, a division of Penguin Books USA Inc. 1990
Published in Penguin Books 1991

3   5   7   9   10   8   6   4   2

"Anthem," "Houw Hoek," and "Sea Lion at Santa Cruz" first
appeared in *Agni Review*; "Arkansas," "Confederate Graveyard:
Franklin, Tennessee," "Medanales," and "Virginia" in *Boulevard*;
"Safed" in *Crazyhorse*; "Fort Worth, Texas" in *Southwest Review*;
"Caesarea," "Capernaum," and "Reddersburg" in *Tikkun*; "For
Tim Sutcliffe" in *TriQuarterly*; "Sabbath: Los Alamos" in *UpStream*;
and "Autumn" in *The Yale Review*.

The Library of Congress has catalogued
the Viking edition as follows:

Sacks, Peter M.
Promised lands/Peter Sacks.
p.   cm.
ISBN 0-670-83176-X (hc.)
ISBN 0 14 058.665 2
I. Title.
PS3569.A235P76   1990
811'.54—dc20   89-40796

Printed in the United States of America

CONTENTS

IV. SEASONS

I.

RETURN

ANTHEM

I.

Home again. The vacant beauty
of False Bay, its wide
blue spanner turning
nothing but the tide,

the haze of fires edging
south as if the colony
had ended, or begun again.
Interrogation and reply,

the hanging scroll of gas;
breathe in, breathe out,
say what you have to say—this thin
damp cloth of words over the mouth.

II.

Subcontinent each
name or rule deforms,
your sandstone giant squats
beyond Good Hope or Storms.

Darkness indivisible,
until a second birth
sets his red face against the skies.
Pressed hard against the earth,

original defeat
outwearing all disguise,
now tears his flesh
but will not fall or rise.

III.

Until the leisure killed him,
slow erosion's pace,
and he invented harder stone,
stone fist, stone face

to smash against the teeth,
the jaw, the skull,
whatever housed the law-abiding
tongue's betrayal.

That fist, carved face nothing can move
he cast from him for our blind
after-search, true mirror, grail.
Said *I'll not bend from this, for any love.*

FOR TIM SUTCLIFFE
(1914–1986)

Headmaster, Clifton
Preparatory School, Durban, South Africa.

Although it's more than twenty years, and though
two weeks had passed before word
of your death, there's always been enough
to draw on, working backward

to the image of you shepherding our parents
on Speech Day—an all-white
school for boys, pre-adolescent
stock of wealthier Durbanites.

A class ritual, you very much headmaster,
large, flushed with the heat, by choice
wearing your Oxford gown, Brasenose, the war.
A radio actor's vivid cast of voice:

"Ladies and gentlemen, boys, I'm happy to . . ."

Inevitably how you flogged me,
the whistle and burning impact of the cane,
I doubled over one arm of an easy
chair, my mouth pressed hard against

the floral pattern of upholstery.
The worst was for disrupting *Hamlet*
at the old Alhambra: had it been only
bravado, the fulfillment of a bet,

or more the overflow of tense desire,
even the fury of self-recognition,
that possessed me to yell "chicken-liver"
when he couldn't stab the king?

Or earlier still, with *Caesar,* how
beneath your voice the world first disappeared
to language—classroom, desks, the glow
of morning light in from the yard

obliterated by the fall of words
that shattered everything except themselves.
You'd clambered dangerously upon two boards
propped on a desk we thought would shelve

beneath your swaying bulk—200 lbs.
packed sweating in a tight safari suit,
like some colonial general in the far bounds
of the tropics. One hand held out,

as if only for balance (since you
hardly looked at it), your copy
of the play, a small blue
Clarendon edition waving open

far above our heads, to Antony
alone with the still bloody corpse
of Caesar. That slow voice of stony
grief and climbing rage forced

me straight into the dark,
as if someone had thrown a switch—
near blackout as the current struck
and held the room.

And do I fix on this, the sheer spell
of annihilating words regardless
of their sense, because an elegy must tell
again the child's first hapless

reaching after syllables; or did I know already
why you chose that speech—the year
of Sharpeville—how the rhetoric of Antony
worked free of time or ideology to bear

the form and pressure of our history?
Hadn't we practiced hiding under desks
the day the crowds marched on the city
carrying rocks and sticks,

as if white children might be trapped at last?
Hard now to disentangle fear
from conscience—had the news passed
by me, just how many had been killed

outside Johannesburg? What was the object
of the anger threatening the room—

the mutilated corpse of Caesar,
or the children shot down in the road;

the bloody hands of Brutus,
or the men with guns? Was it the frenzy
of *all* civil war, contagion of the blood about us
with the prophecy already

shadowing the land? "O pardon me,
thou bleeding piece of earth, that I
am meek and gentle with these butchers . . ."
the utterance pouring out like blood indeed,

more than a turn of phrase,
already gathering, brutal, eloquent,
unstoppable, to the appalling
fury of the curse, the spirit calling

for revenge "with Até by his side
come hot from hell" (by now you'd worked
inside the raging ghost) "shall in these confines
with a monarch's voice cry 'Havoc!'

and let slip the dogs of war. . . ."
—Impossible to say now what was understood,
how much was sense, and what was naked terror
molded only later into sorrow,

conscience, rage—with fear still
at the heart. Twenty-five years since,

that same fear draws me back to school—
that and desire for the mastery of voice

now that you're gone. Rest where you are
beyond the red trench of our land;
leave us what you once gave—
if not the power to revenge,

then strength to name those whom to curse,
and those for whom to save our hearts,
to carry as from war
toward an unknown peace.

MEMORIAL

I.   Rhodes

Shouldering the rock above
this slope of foreign pine;
a cold prospector's gaze
over the continent he'd mine.

Delirium of empire, past
the bow or spear;
blood sheathing mineral,
your hinterland is there.

II.   *Die Stem*

Burgers, Boers, Voortrekkers
from a foreign crown,
unfairly broken by an old empire
until we came into our own.

Brooding dominations
of the blood and tongue,
still singing *Ons vir jou*
until the stones approve our song.

Past reason or remorse
we chew the toughened hope
of our survival—red meat
twisted to a hard black rope.

10

III.   Day of the Covenant
       16.xii.1986

Northeast of Pretoria, in bush
country, hyenas chew the head
of a young hippo stranded
neck-deep in a marsh.

Heavier predators will not
risk the mud; there's no
clean death, only this slow
feasting. A sure start

at the ears, then stripping,
gnawing, grinding through
the unfleshed skull, until they
rip into the brain. In a ring

the adults, careful of their young,
inspect the circling terrain,
rest, then eat again.
One grips the red stump of the tongue.

REDDERSBURG

for my father

Note: Reddersburg ("town of the Savior"), a small
village in the Orange Free State, South Africa.

New Year's Day. The journey to your childhood
home dragged hours out of schedule
by our breakdowns on the road
west from Natal;

already too late for your boarding school
(among the places I'd requested),
no talk now of coming back, of how "you'll
see it next time you come out."

Driving slowly through the red swirl
of an Orange Free State dust-storm,
Bloemfontein by nightfall,
the "flower-fountain" at the scorched

heart of our country—trash
blown through the empty streets,
car rocked by the hot wind, map
uncrumpled on your knees,

I peering for the sign to Reddersburg,
swerving past torn tumbleweed,
each bush caught dead-white
in the high beam of our lights.

The Sarie Marais Hotel: thin corridor,
pegboard walls, no water after dark.

12

Too late even for the bar,
we bled the pipes a cupful at a time,

enough to rinse away the sweat,
though all that night the wind drove sand
through window-cracks, pink drapes, the sheets.
I woke, grit between my teeth,

to look out at the semi-desert town
surrounded by "but *nothing*," as you said
with chronic emphasis. Your birth-place
like a broken callus on the plain.

Dirt streets, gaunt iron windmills,
low veranda cottages on blocks,
the park for Boet Coetzee—dry scrub
circling a monumental lump of rock.

Low-voiced, with the deliberate style
I'd overheard recording diagnoses after work,
you dictated memories to a small
recorder, as we passed the *Dopperkerk*

you'd watched Italian masons building
stone by stone between the wars;
a dark garage and blacksmith stall; the old
drankwinkel with its bottles behind bars;

rebuilt within its compound of new wire,
the squat police station still edging town
at the corner of Boshof and Beyer.
Only the jail's unimproved, the same stone

blockhouse you remembered, calling it
die tronk to savor the hard grip
of rock and iron, the Afrikaans word
fastened to its root.

A typical location for such buildings, set
to guard the white town from its shadow
flung out on the veld
a mile away—a snarl of yellow

footpaths disappearing into coalsmoke, dust—
like all black encampments in this country,
isolated well enough to cut the tenants off
from killing any but themselves.

You never liked such talk. Too mild
yourself for bitterness; perhaps too strong,
a stubborn strength that turned from what
you couldn't change, crossed with an instinct

for what nourishes, the almost liquid softness
of a man whose favorite word is *rugged.*

I'm trying to adjust that mixture
in myself, remembering the small house

you were born in, wooden rooms,
the lights on pulleys weighted down with shot,
a front stoop now enclosed, you recollecting
what was gone—the upright piano,

a cooling-box of coal and chickenwire;
you spoke of kosher meat brought in by post-car
six hours from the railway line;
your mother's cleanliness, fanatical

as any prejudice (vacations home began
with castor oil to purge the *tref*),
her nervous clutch on the familiar
broken only by migrations, deaths—

the same grip I could barely tell
from love or fortitude years later
in the Home; one hand held soft
yet rigid as a dead bird in the other.

I bought a tin mug at the trading store
your father owned before they moved away—
a Lithuanian refugee among the Boers,
his Yiddish mixing into Afrikaans,

the daily Talmud crossing
with tough sheep-farmers' lore;
not tough enough to save
his own farm in the drought.

Each July they'd winter with us at the coast.
I still hear him beat time on the table
as he *dovened* after dinner; strong almost
as prayer itself, an image now of iron

wrapped in cloth. One Friday night
outside the *shul,* I caught his fingers
in the car door: so softly he said "my fingers,"
so gently—the words repeated twice

before I understood. Cut hand reddening
a handkerchief, he sat through services
as if unhurt. As if religion
took the place of arbitrary pain.

Since the last drought, little's grown
except the cemetery. The old names,
Beyer, Boshof, Van der Walt,
cut deep on horizontal slabs,

the ground too hard for any flowers
but imitation petals
of rough porcelain. Once globed
in cheap glass, shattered now—

tin leaves, jagged petals,
shards of glass caught
in a nest of rusted stems—
a brittle crater baked on every grave.

In a small plot of their own,
a handful of young soldiers
killed *For King and Empire*
somewhere in the empty plain:

Irving, Murphy, Dimsdale,
buried among their enemies—
the Boer War still a hard stone
in the belly of this nation.

All your life you've known the blue void
over long, undeviating roads, "as if you could
look straight into forever," the sun
sledge-hammering the veld, bleached earth,

gray-green furze, sharp stones.
Signs of what you came to trust,
a standard of reality I've not known
this clearly until now,

discovering here something congenital,
the core of a resistant strength
that calms me, obdurate and loyal
against my drifting ease,

yet terrifies—an image of the fixity
now shattering the country;
or the stone heart of a personal regime
that turns away from each

new headline of detention, death,
knowing no words, however chosen,
that may change or break
the will of those who rule,

yet praying, neither for inherited
belief nor patience,
but for a persistence as of anger
hardening the hope that listens

for a sound—improbable, warm, and vehement
as the rain, heard falling evenly
beyond the one clear ring of steel,
chiseling memorials for what it could not save.

HOUW HOEK

for my mother

A narrow mountain valley damp with rain,
the trees near dormancy—Cape apples
I've not eaten since I came away,
Starking, Starcrimson, Winter Pearmain;
thin branches strung on wires,
the fruit withdrawn to another world.

My own unseasonable returns,
irregular Persephone gathering
dry words for the memory of rain,
the wooded slope we climbed above the inn's
old buildings half-seen dwindling under oaks,
the single blue gum's cataract of leaves.

Crossing to higher grasses, flowering heather,
leucodendrons opening their tough yellow flame,
bright everlastings, paling as they dry.
Your childhood valley—though how speak of beauty now,
or tell of death and quick reblossoming,
as if all suffering were just, and justice beautiful?

What of the radical sweetness
of a child's love for its mother—
body-cradled before language, law,
the sure absorption of that sap
still rising through the marrow against
whatever rule has held us separate, alone?

How else speak of the motherland
but through the loosening beneath all words,

19

of honey oozing in the cell, wild seed
cramming every pitted boulder
on the slopes around us, new growth
shivering in the fresh salt air?

Gashed sweetness here—grafted to the blind
uncoiling drive to smash into the treasuries
of greater love, past anger, old division,
hacking deep into the vats—a shadow mouth's
forbidden mumblings of milk and origin,
the salt, the egg, the rocking sack of blood.

Mother, *matria,* palace of wheat and honey,
pillar of the orchard, tent of peace:
take back your children, meager,
bitter, and unkind; take back
the unrecovered dead and the unborn;
take back the broken land.

II.

IN THE HIGH PLACES
OF THE FIELD

GALILEE

On Tabgha's cracked church floor
fish and bread recall the miracle
that all but satisfied the poor.

Downshore an old lifesaver stows
his rescue board, but keeps a wire
basket of St. Peters flapping in the shallows,

raising them to buyers, who decline
the small fish leaping now less quickly
as they're set back in the fretted shine.

I think too late of buying the entire
catch, uncaged to ripple free,
a bright net shaken out, each fish no larger

than the hands of a late swimmer wading
lit with dying silver to the shore.
Near naked, half-afloat, half-treading,

each step heavier at the water's edge:
what mosaic token, coin, or chariot
would buy my crossing past all knowledge

of this country, hard yet broken
like an olive stump still buried in the soil?
As if I grew from nothing I recall.

CAPERNAUM

A synagogue above the sea,
white stone pediments
scattered like objects of a curse.

This chunk of lintel with its ark,
a temple-wagon's crooked wheels
failing their load—

eroded to a purity beyond
the carver's need to resurrect
the faith of fugitives, the desert light,

the creak of wheels under a wandering law.
Still led by smoke and fire,
as if a chisel could bring back

the wilderness they circled,
blown dust clinging to the holy stones.
The souvenir impossible to tell from prophecy.

TIBERIAS

This too, the actual Galilee,
cool green waters where Christ
called Peter and Andrew
to the narrow ledge of a new life,

the sure pursuit of immortality
held firmly as the heavy net
they once let down into the sea.
No living savior,

no call but the dry wind's
rasp over the waters,
channeling a smoky light
against the stone of the Golan;

my breath less than the breath
of those who've fallen on the heights,
an irritable wind that whips
between the watchtowers and wire

to mar the flight of this small bird
I call a Syrian dove. Quick dipping,
dusty rose, it drinks from the lake
as lamps are lit, flies upward

veering hard against the globe above me,
snapping wing or neck to drop unmoving,
one wing awkwardly extended
for the quick flight of recovery.

I too, motionless.
Repeating like a broken spell:
day turns to night,
hope to its dark twin, hope.

SAFED

Note: the Ari, popular name
for Rabbi Isaac Luria (1534–1572).

Where they believed and saw, more than
a mirror in the world of separation,
stars and other garments, letters,
crowns, even the branches of dead trees

invested with the light of God,
the daily token of redemption
sinking like a burning coin
behind the far slope of Meron.

As it does now, black coats
fluttering to the Ari's tomb,
blue paint blackened by the soot
of candles wriggling in a jar,

Zaddik crudely painted on tin signs,
the righteousness that cometh from afar.
—And that we come to this same grave
as if it promised holy speech,

the composition of a ghost or angel
pieced together by our shaping of the air;
forgetting that his faith, the warning
against sorrow, anger that can tear

the soul like cloth, was fastened
to its version of despair,
perpetuation of an exile
that would not be ended in the Holy Land.

For which he rose at midnight to lament
the temple and the bride, reciting psalms of loss:
How long? and *Yea we wept.* . . .
For which he ate wild grass,

even thistles and thorns,
to take upon himself the curse
no chirping bird or fragment of an evening
prayer can temper, as the hour

turns toward its sternest attribute.
And I walk aimlessly toward the new town,
stopping at the cinema's projection room
left open to the street, the blue beam

falling to a bloody war in space:
a human hero in dark armor
battling planetary troops
clad in such brilliance

they must have been the Sons of Light,
and he . . . before I'm asked to leave.
Drawn on by wedding music
to the basement of a new hotel,

the bride enthroned like a colossal
lump of wax already melting
under video lamps; pink chaise
shimmering about her satin and gauze,

the groom behind her,
dogged, soldierly, aloof,
guests bending for a quick peck
at the cheek—self-conscious,

shielding their eyes against the glare
that leaves me near blind
in a stretch of unlit street,
colliding with a soldier on patrol,

both peering downward to avoid
the cobbles torn up for repair.
—O Luria, your vision of wrecked vessels
and the long work of return,

how should our hands and voices
marry yet again the broken pair,
Compassion and His Kingdom,
now, before our human work is done?

The startled soldier mutters "Pardon"
with an angry smile, still looking downward
as he walks toward the lights,
reshouldering the short stub of his gun.

CAESAREA

Beyond the parking lot, another emperor
lifts his spoiled face
to yet another layer of salt.

Stone tunnels of the *vomitoria*—
even sea wind over water-basins
couldn't cool the magistrates:

this by lion, these by amputations
as the army tested a new sword.
And each day's popular finale,

hundreds daubed with resin
wrist to wrist, a human fuse
that burned toward a single flame.

One might still smell it in the air,
but for the reek of fishing bait
blown into the arena;

still hear echoes of their cries,
but for the shredded song
of a young pilgrim singing to his group,

a weak voice lifting to the wind
some milky song of Jesus—and with growing
confidence if nothing else, "Amazing Grace."

But when Akiba was led forth
it was the hour to recite the *Shema,*
so that after the Romans

raked his flesh with iron combs,
each tooth sharpened well enough
to rip the stomach and throat,

his last breath lengthened out
the final word of testament,
until both Jews and Romans

heard a voice descending,
*Hail to Akiba, who has given
his spirit to the final One.*

And Eleazar, last to die,
saw as he was nailed to the ground
the souls of the righteous cleansing

in the waters of Shiloah, preparing
for Akiba's teaching in the seventh palace,
to which even the angels brought their chairs.

—As who would not believe?
Or wish to—even the "decaying scribe,"
so-called already in Akiba's time,

who sitting in the warm sea wind
that will not purify, however hard
it blows against these stones,

rewrites or cancels yet another
passage of the Law—
something of sacrifice, or daily butchery:

And when the meat is white,
Even the veins of it,
Scrape off the salt.
Scrape off the bloody salt.

MEGIDDO

Above the gates of Solomon,
the chariots of Ahab,
vanished under thistle, under shard,
the sun burns in a blind stone manger
—even my hand, pulled back into the shade,
has left the flaring image
of its palm against the stone.

A black jet wheels over Nazareth,
and each horizon doubles the low thunder
—Josiah in his chariot, dragged
back to Jerusalem, an armored corpse;
the seventh angel pouring out its vial.

A place called Armageddon in the Hebrew tongue,
where nothing holds a candle to the glare
but thistles, withered and irregular,
their small crowns giving back
the lowest color of the flame;
where still, through its cool fault,
the clear spring water runs under the hill.

JERUSALEM

I. JOSEPHUS

Throat-sore, yelling upward,
Save yourselves! The temple!
Pelted, scoffed at even by the doomed
(already scavenging grass, old dung),
he parleyed, offered guarantees
—until they let a pig out of the walls.

So he saved his breath,
recorded what he saw:
in search of coins, the Romans
gutted those caught fleeing after dark;
he watched the sentries
slitting through intestines in the firelight.

As he had warned,
the silver melted from the temple doors,
streets ran like open veins,
and every corner had its corpse.
When he was done,
he threw his sandals in the fire.

And still we read you,
Roman Joseph,
as a lawyer reads the law.
Turncoat, witness,
undertaker.
History's faithful whore.

II.

Each captive holds this city
like a stone shell to the ear.
Only the blood's return
keeps it whispering there:

Was there no city built for love,
no sacrifice for joy,
the singer-king who bound me
was once a shepherd boy.

Come, put off my girdle,
tear the winding sheet;
for offering lay down your pride,
the red steps at my feet.

III.

City of scabbed shellac,
your walls burn over us;
we are the butchered ox
that sees you whole.

Encrusted limestones
rupturing their blood,
gold tar of faith,
torched honeycomb.

35

Elegies for
The Promised Land

I.

This was our pasturage,
thick crop of tar's emulsion
where the heart drips in its red nest
like a fallen torch.

Past sacrifice or harvest
at the field's edge
the guardian pours its thundering
river-tree of meat.

II.

Seething coffin,
horse and rider crumbled to rose marl,
pennants like sea serpents
coupling on the tides.

Over the desert glare
a gray cloud's melting brain,
the photographic flame
of raw-red Moses hacking out the slag.

III.

To your black bracket
in the low arch of the kiln
Shulamit we have brought
a remnant of the seventh flame.

This wrist-thin stump
of tallow, weeping smoke
over the burned-out
quarry of the heart.

IV.

So this is peace,
the olive twig and its dry leaf
stapled to the iron cross.

Tangled tracks
cross over, swing apart
to swarm the camps of night;

near carbonized,
the yellow lions glare
and lick their hearts.

V.

Singer, savior, silver mouth
still gaping from the fence,
this is your afterlife,
who once called on the king of kings.

Starlit fingers rust into the wire.
Beneath your crown
the same disasters stare,
and stare us down.

III.

STATES

For these states tend inland and toward the Western sea, and I will also.
—Whitman

VIRGINIA

"Earth's only paradise"

Scoff and slap of water on the old sea wall,
charred stumps of the colony—survival
bent to greed, betrayal, open trenches
of the Civil War cut deep between the trees.

Wet clay clinging to our boots,
we stood below an early star
we'd not have seen had not the geese
swept by it at the edge of dark . . .

echoes of their wings and hollow cries,
a long migration, with the single star
to recollect an image of the soul
set free of any constellation.

But as we stared out at the later skies,
the lit stone of the moon half-sunk
to shadows shifting in the dim beanfield,
a blind unbroken will bound everything

—even a large buck crashing heavily
through low branches, swerving back unseen,
caught here for all its freedom
no less than ourselves, the geese in flight,

the fields streaming under them—all held
however dark and drifting, like the nailed
club of Orion, turning with him as he rises
headless in the open door of night.

41

VETERANS DAY:
WASHINGTON, D.C.

From the gold crown of a maple
breaks a crow's hard cry;
and then again, a mirror cracking,
though it's only beauty
mortified, and only nature's cry.

Beyond the city, white stones
block the barrows of our empire,
severed hands
that buried other hands
yet deeper in the mire.

Who would be mute
for ceremony take these stumps
home to the mouth.
How else stifle
the red name of history,

since none of us,
so called, and called,
can match the hard
unchoking answer
of a natural cry.

BUCKS COUNTY,
PENNSYLVANIA

High, unharvested, the dry corn
grinning in its sheaths,

amber-pebbled amulets
one might turn in one's pocket

at a change of season
or sudden flock of birds.

At dusk a wavering white tail
flags the evergreens,

a car passing too fast for any call
beyond the squeal and thud—a deer down,

hind legs scrabbling asphalt,
head still riding freely

as the driver tiptoes round the ear,
the deer half-reared above unbroken forelegs

struggling to shake free
haunches, shattered spine.

The land itself drawn off,
an ocean at low tide:

"Came out of nowhere, out of nowhere!"
he kept saying like a prayer.

The old myth dying hard
—the garden, innocence again.

Where else could it come from?

CONFEDERATE GRAVEYARD:
FRANKLIN, TENNESSEE

As if during a civil war we praised
only the wooded hills declining to a field,
the leaves releasing their last shimmer
to the wind, the slatted light
cut through a barn—as if these
signaled anything except by contraries.

All day I've thought of one who turned
from coffins in the road to call
on honeybees to build where starlings
once had nested in the loosening wall;
yet even he, to purge his bitterness,
was driven to unnatural images of joy.

Out of what hope, believing only
in what little earth remains to know
seedtime and harvest, out of what fidelity
return to count these birds and thistles
marking the barley where eight thousand soldiers
killed each other in a day?

The open field beyond the wall, the cedars
shadowing the stones, even the ash-blue pellets
scattered underfoot, cannot compose
or minister to each revulsion of the heart:
as rainfall soaks into the poisonable earth,
we soak into the dead. How rise?

ARKANSAS

The darker body of the hawk
against its wings—
almost the figure of a man
outspread against the fringes of his body
lifting him into a web of light.

Bent head, hooded, sharpening,
the sweep of arms,
the torso dense, condensed
by speed and hunger
to such concentration of the flesh

the soul unsheathes
into the arrow-flight
of predator already
shadowing its prey—
past nourishment,

beyond even the purifying
of its flight—
the shattering catastrophe
that takes it home
into the dark.

Asleep in West Memphis,
I saw a red-haired
woman throwing bottles at a wall.
And as they shattered, shaking out the fire
of her hair, she chanted

"I know the Power,
I *am* the Power!"
—the massive image of her rising free
above the close folds of the Ouachitas,
the shoulder of the Ozarks,

hovering above the highway
hideous with the wreckage
of small tortoises, the broken shell
above each pool of blood—red meat
under the careful jigsaw

of protection—slow
accommodations of the tender
and the tough, flesh and its covering,
the timeless caution of the eyes,
the furtive risk and purpose of the neck,

smashed past all healing.
—Now, as the childhood
fantasy revives of stretching
from the car to hold the skull
against the speeding surface of the road,

revives also an image
as of muteness
breaking into flight,
even the purest flight of words
with their small weight

47

of shadowy compressions,
crushing and disfiguring
past all care of beauty, to the mark
where they have struck against
what will not break.

O white shell of the world,
O walls, O flame-red chant of power,
do not lay me down
in sweet catalpa,
sassafras or cypress

such as grow on these high hills.
Do not bury me in hardwoods,
hickory or ash.
O do not bury me.
O do not lay me down into the earth!

FORT WORTH, TEXAS

I. BILLY BOB'S

How all originals bleed through
thinning layers of superimposition
—time, forgetfulness, revision—
light from a dead star neither you

nor I, caught in this later atmosphere,
have miracles to redeem.
That cowboy riding his high dream,
returning beyond fear

to the first motion
stirring under him before the fall
—eight seconds of a caul
ripped from the wild extension

of a body not his own, whose every jolting
thrash beneath him his one
grace and prize depends on
driving to the limits of revolt.

Small wonder we watch only
the hand that does not grip, its flinging
governed by the massive seething
under it, that without penalty

may touch neither the rider nor the bull
—a scrap of flesh now flying dragged

half-trapped, half-free as any flag
for what is ours and yet escapes us all.

II. DUCCIO, KIMBELL ART MUSEUM

Or take this cattle trough the painter
first laid down for Lazarus' tomb,
an oblong of pink stone whose rim
now pushes its reminder

through the bandaged thighs, the body still
wrapped in its cerements,
propped like a board against the entrance
to a blood-dark cavity in the hill.

Or how the lid shows through the arm
of one who holds it, almost an embrace,
the crowd locked to the greenish face
of Lazarus reviving, though beneath the balm

as even Martha said, he must
have stunk—a young man shielding his nose,
caught now forever in that pose
between sheer wonder and disgust.

—Like Lazarus himself. Bound hand and foot,
dragged from the marvel of his death
to this excruciating stir of breath,
returning blood, to face again the brute

uncaged animal, the domineering voice
Loose him and let him go, announcing
yet another miracle. And he renouncing
in a glaring land beyond all choice

(unable even to control his legs)
that perfect home and one true
shade for which, as he now knew,
even the Devil begs.

ARIZONA

Gliding through the stone jaws
of a side canyon
to moor in the still
water of a narrow green lagoon,
no path uphill
but the debris of a dry water-course.

Granite boulders, red blocks
carved from the walls, a wash
of dead trees flung
aside like trash,
the jawbone of a young
goat blazing on the rocks.

Silence, gravel parks
of a deserted town
after the waters disappeared,
amphitheaters, basins of smooth stone
where only heat ripples
against old water marks.

Deeper in the defile,
both walls, lit and shadowed,
wedge to a ladder of loose rock.
Clambering, squeezing upward
through a chimney to the shock
of a glittering pool

set thirty feet below where limestone
meets bright angel shale;
the water forced to drip
outward between impermeable
and softer stone, a fern lip
slowing the deliberate rain.

To slip into the pool, to drift
half-stroking back across
the water, looking up between
each sphere of light hung motionless
in its descent, until this
looking is a steady lift

beyond the cast-off coil
of skin, flesh, skeleton
scattered back down-canyon
in a twisting corridor of bone.
As if this brilliant fall had drawn
the rising waters of the soul.

MEDANALES,
NEW MEXICO

for Barbara

Now as the bare intensity
of light clings burning the side
of this thin cottonwood, accentuating every
groove, the brittle individuality
of every branch, even the shadows eating deep
into the carved bark of the tree,

a blur of reddish liquid
squeezes from a downturned leaf,
detaches outward in the air—
a butterfly identified
in just the pulse and a half
it takes to disappear.

Beyond the trees, you're painting
the last light, the field already
shadowed, darkness on a row
of Russian olives climbing
the near hills, an early
snow light on the Sangre de Cristo.

And I remember climbing the arroyo
at a later sunset, looking back
toward the barn, the west side in full glow
around the black cube of a door
in which I saw you moving back
and forth, a lighter shade within the shadow.

You were sanding panels for an overlay
of white that would become
the ground, to cast light upward
through the paint, eventually
transparent as it ages, even the umbers
and violets used for shade.

The sun was level with the barn, and seeing
you framed that way, I said
though out of hearing, wait for me in that place,
the clarity that age may bring;
and in the night that will have gathered
round us—sheer and severing.

SABBATH:
LOS ALAMOS

From a small apple orchard
with the last sun flowing through the yellow
trees as if the fruit,
worm-eaten, bruised against the hard
branches, still hung within a sunlit
Palestine four centuries ago,

I too face the black hills of the west,
cover my heart,
and offer what—praise,
gratitude, belief? At best
the shaken branches
of remember and observe.

If I could recognize both
angels I would walk between
them to the house,
sing welcome to the Sabbath
and the exiled queen
still blind with loss.

Sing come, return;
as if this could well
be the time of union and of peace,
when the Ancient and Impatient One,
He of the narrow face,
keeps out the dogs of hell.

SEA LION
AT SANTA CRUZ

for Barbara—
on the loss of a favorite earring

The long jetty at night, half bridge
to nowhere, wedge posts sunk
into the blackened suck and welling;
jittery lamplight spelling everything
we couldn't see: near everything.

And then a gasp and heaving bellow
as the sea broke its own
fluencies to moaning cries,
a sea lion peering back at us,
two unwrapped coals igniting in the shallows

as the lamplight struck and mirrored
its own brightness in the shifting eyes.
But while we hung there following
their mineral gleam, your earring
slipped and disappeared before

we caught more than its after-image,
silver, turquoise, gone . . .
And unaware, the sea lion still
bellowing "Feed me! Feed me!
Don't just lead me on!"

Centuries ago, a ritual might
have brought two lovers to the same night sea:
the hollow voice, the eyes returning

torchlight with the burning chill
the couple had been told

would meet them in the waves. The vow,
one of two figurines untwinned,
cast spinning to her keeping
who would keep as one all
pairs that let such tribute fall.

But love, our offerings are inexact,
the best too costly to be meant.
And who should we suppose sent to receive them?
—Your earring's gone. The sea lion
hasn't the vaguest notion

of what dropped past his hunger. Take
in exchange for our sake only
the unearthly glance that took
us home to its cold flame; that shifts
beyond our need to make all losses gifts.

WRECK BEACH, CALIFORNIA

. . . *his blood will I require*
at the watchman's hand.
Ezekiel 33:6

Gold dust, umbels of the California laurel
trodden to a path. Beneath the cliffs, the rolling mower's
sword-bright scatterings, welded to the plough.

These are the spoils of peace,
the western chariots rusting on the red sea roads.
Who wouldn't anchor here after the tide's return

—transparent silt, the cordage
stiffening between real loss, imaginary gain?
Torn backward and away, cries

echo in the backwash of worn shells
thou art no more than as a lovely song
they hear thy words and yet they do them not.

Thin residues, bled free,
the lining of the watchman's hand
held out for payment, not for prophecy.

Beyond the waves the sea loosens its prey.
Ungainly birds swarm, falling, rising,
gorging till they have outweighed their wings.

ALASKA

Long he must stammer in his speech;
often forgo the living for the dead.
Emerson

Old questions of a given land here change their form,
unravel, swim away, press back with muffled pressure
garbled in the water—rungs of a decaying ladder
rotted into separation, swaying in the current
like ungathered weed, pulled deeper into looming versions
of the light that fractures in unquiet waters,
globed, impenetrable, warped past recognition—
all once hallowed vanishings become mere bloatings,
old decompositions found then lost again
as dead fish turn and return in the water light.

~

And so he slept. The water took him down,
no breath for anger, none for cowardice,
green castles reddening.

How to call on God when he could hear
only the staggered thunder of his heart
redoubling through the blood-warm belly of the sea?

Driftwood, rotting lumber, slimey weed like bell ropes
tangled into relics of the ancient world,
Tarshish and Nineveh.

Who washes out the blood of prophets,
washed out to indifference?
Blue coins whitening above the hulks,
the words *Beloved, Justice,* shadowing.

60

Thy billows and thy waves passed over me.

~

Tall ghosts and herring-bones look down between the pines.
Above the waterways a last tin roof sails through the trees;
the wind has blown the light to a clear polish
and it falls around us now, a glitter of debris.

Seen from below, dark facets of sea surface labor home
—a wing, down bright, up caught in its own shade.

Now that I cannot breathe give me that wing for breath!
The fishtail of the Bella Coola mask disfiguring the mouth:

to hear that early voice flung to the winding channels
of the air—the skein of it unraveling.

~

Near blind from gathering the light, look down
through layers undersea—the nations welded into combat,
men in trenches, tangled in the wire.

The same flesh turns to bloody smoke, caught
hanging in thin strings above the towers and trees.

Below, the limbless shadows slip
across the floor to the high oven of Troy.
Scamander running red into the sea.

No visionary cycle ordered in the mind,
only the chaos of what's glimpsed
while sinking, sway and countersway,
the sea-bent glimmer of disaster.

Farther down, whales drift and roll
their barrels over the Hesperides;
look down from the weak glamour of the grail
bulging with borrowed light

to the marled ark, square beams under the sail,
the bones of Noah, who would not intercede.

Still hung in curdling dust, the later patriarch:
I'll do this in the sleep we call obedience
whose seed would multiply.

Generations climbing the stone ladder of Moriah
think only of that motion, stalled, released:
pull back the arm, let fall the bright edge of the knife.

And now the current flowing east between low willows,
unstrung wires like smoke uncoiling through the leaves.

~

Salt hangs low above the hills of a remembered land;
merely to walk brings tears. We have forgotten everything,
never to see the backs of our right hands. Like thirst,
the need to memorize a new song of these waters.

Farther off, a long swell breaks upon itself,
a white sign thrown backward on the wake—
the black map of the sea.

We mock ourselves who thought of words we might have sung
together, steps worn glassy with long use,
thin leaves dragged sideways in the current.

Of happiness, of cradled joy; and of the shining
jewels of revenge, the children broken on the stones.

Across the Passage of Grace, below the scars left burning
in the light, a gray barge tows the body of the Lord,
the cedars, spruce, *O do not lay me down,*
the broken shell and body of the Lord.

~

The mountains were of another world,
snow-capped where snow could hold the rock,
a deeper blue than any shadow of this world.

And let the voice come down,
come through the ragged opening of the tent:

these scales of water lift toward him in their praise,
and let the hearts turn back,

the hearts of those who waste us
turn, O Lord . . . *who waste us.*

~

Stone wing of the mountain.
Harder than a cure for time, a change of heart.

Through ash the sun trains its one eye toward us:
the waters fall back as we pass.

For there had been light upon the waters,
and the memory of light at evening bannering the sails;

mouths opened on the surface of the sea,
a song of beaten gold that vanished as they sang
the waters fall back as we pass.

~

Below the glacier wall brown water stains the bay,
the shrouded cold on which we floated,
out of which we sailed.

Between the midnight and the dawn I saw the whales
turning—flick and slow subsidence of the tail,

the dark hulks following to save
And canst thou bind the influences
canst thou loose the bands?

And where is that Leviathan of pride,
breaker of anchors, hooks and old harpoons,
for whom all iron is straw, and brass is rotten wood?

~

Something of earliness,
first syllables, old bonds and covenants.
The soul's revulsion at the tawdry will.

Returning words *all pity chok'd . . . how can we sing*
. . . Orion headless in the door of night,
the rags of icebergs,
wreckage of an unseen highness in the icy bounds.

The blind unbroken will.

~

Yellow light seeps out across the farthest water,
light under a closing door, clouds streaming off the planet,
rivers off the land. Already how the blood-light

sparkles on unbroken waves—still rising, falling
deeper to a ceremonious descent,
or is it climbing to the throne, the marble stairs?

Think back to half-seen ships *there go the ships*
before sunrise, the west streaked orange, citron, ash,
a light wind on the radar pressing in
against another field of force.

~

They've melted down the metal of the bells
to faceless coins. We float beneath them
free to forge our own insignia. To choose
and cast away: the chariot, the palm, the lion's head.
The face of an imagined king.

And here, long after our defeat,
the coin of coins without horizon,
every lesser recollection fallen out of mind.

The coin turns through the water, passes through the body
pummeled slowly, widening, until there is no coin
but the surrounding sea.
As if our ransom had been everywhere!

~

Circling power through thin fringes of the fog
the drifting meadows of the air

soon after death to come on other words
like sea birds pushing upward from the sea,
the red feet of a guillemot folding into flight.

—To have this swept aside, panels of air pulled
backward as a greater bird tears from the waves,
high wings of water streaming outward,
feathers burning at the verge of sight:

I see you all in this wide emptiness,
the clean and the corrupt, I see you all
who have despaired of your conversion.

Now that a voice commands above the torn face of the sea,
refuse the evil, choose the good, who would obey?
And who would ask for guarantees,
dew on the fleece, and then the fleece left dry?

Your asking as I hover over you is your despair,
corrosion of the soul—of justice nothing but the shadow,
sacrifice only the bright edge of the knife.

~

How each swell builds, subsides or turns upon itself
to break; behind a face of shadowed water
fragments of white lace fall back and fall away.

We're carried sideways as the sea gives way around us.
Long dissolved, the drawbridge of lit water
where we saw the wings, the ladder rungs and bells
long sunken out of sound.

Until even the angel vanishes, upheld
a moment in the wake of each unsatisfying phrase,
the black map of the sea accelerations of mad fluency
to which we put no name, each dissolution
caught between relenting and returning to the break,

the sudden shattering of shells, half-open mouths
What of Leviathan, the slant serpent? What of Leviathan?

~

Between destruction and redemption
we who know nothing of purity except the word
move through the waters,
move into the fire no breath can name,
the fire that will not say *it is enough*

until we breathe again.

IV.

SEASONS

It is curious that the physical
order of things is so slow to filter
down into us, and then so impossible
to drain back out. But what of the rest?
—Montale

WINTER

1.

Tonight a portion of the wasting moon rose
red as heresy returning from the world,
as if some other fruit, unseen till now,
hung on the scaffold of the tree—
a north wind gathering the orchard into ice.

And when that spirit blows,
the spirit of the perishable world,
it brings the winter
and the winter is the world.

2.

A life still folded at the crease of exile
flashing back the motherland like sunset on the ice,
frozen palms, flamboyants hung with swords.

Cold effigies, lie back into the stone,
it is the season of indifference,
of lovelessness beneath the whistling flute;
a novice conjuring the reptile or the desert wolf,
an adolescent god made old, frigid at heart.

3.

This is our bondage, that we build
the image of undying kings,

the crystal and corona high above the tomb,
the basalt boat with its deep lid of stars.

Until we've grown old among our enemies:
leafless, each tree black as charcoal,
the impatient sketch becomes the will of what survives,
carbon flashing in the light of shorter days,
the diamond and its leaves.

And though such flourishes of hard
unearthly light wait sheathed in repetitions
of each season, I drew back from seeing
past and future fall to the same ash,

who in the quarry laughed
to hear a prince of our own blood
would lead us to the desert—
some said for the week of sacrifice,
while others muttered of a Promised Land.

4.

They said give form to what uncoils,
the body of a snake still filmed with mucus,
blinking back the light

—who knows nothing of us, is older,
will outlive us; though that night
I saw a young snake struck and mangled by a car,

three inches of intestine covering
green-gold diamonds of the skin,
head twisting, mouth-side up, gasping for air,
the jaw unhinged to swallow its own death.

5.

Oppression stiffening to art,
the flowing muscle hardened to a rod.
A season of forbidden prayer, in which devotion,
long suppressed, had made a ritual of each accident;
until whatever happened or was conjured,
caught within that need, contracted, hard, opaque,
became a mirror for the god.

6.

Smoke fills the valley air:
beyond the chimney's flame
a longing for the natural world returns—

before moonrise, the ragged lines of geese,
their underwings and bellies flushed with light,
long broken lines in early spring, wavering

bewildered to the north, and to the frozen west,
caught now, for the first time,
by more than their instinctual flight.

SPRING

1.

Before dawn, birdcalls
from the scarlet oak,
too dark to see the bird,
only a depression of the branch;
my window sibyl singing
wake and *wake and go.*

2.

Sunrise and the broken seed,
for which we pour again
spring water and the cloying wine,

for which we dip and mumble
the unleavened bread of exodus,
betrayal and return,
reddened earth mixed with the breaking rain.

Who holds us in the hand?
Who casts us out?
What sower casting seed midstride
above the channel of engendering?

O dark mouth singing in the trench,
beneath the soft green mask of April,
white May blossom and sweet rain:

74

reopening each black socket in the earth,
who takes us home?

3.

Why ask, if not to pray,
as leaves uncurl,
hands of the infant opening?

Whose are we that devise
our own way now
of bringing on the end,

who walk this season looking backward,
as the dead might summon images of birth,
to our first table

set with parsley, blackened bone,
this ritual numbering—
a drop of wine for every plague?

4.

As if we hadn't been the passing angel
and the families below,
the damned and the bewildered,
daubs of panic smeared before the blood could dry.

As if I hadn't drawn back:
for every life now bound more tightly to the wheel,

a shadow slipping out alone toward the dream
of an unbloodied state beyond necessity,

uplifted waters spilling from their shell
to wash the last reflection of the body
in a shower of celestial rain,
the leaves suspended freely on the tree.

5.

This is the language of an old evasion
(*wake and go, go where you will,*
martyrdom no more than a mistaken witness of the flesh,
and tyranny a shadow cast against the wall).

Now only flaws collect that early brilliance,
the mullion scar in which the light grows solid.

Nothing is released or given back
until the glass is smashed,
the burning sand drifts back into the air.

High in the oak, the goldfinch
moves in memory, late-nesting, migrant,
startled into flight, its sharp cry
altered but irrevocable.

6.

And so they followed fire and smoke
until a murmuring generation
vanished in the sands.

A nation of weak fugitives
recast by war,
the homeland stolen field by field,

even the high stone city of the king
—until these too had ripened on the tree.

SUMMER

1.

This is the heat of our captivity,
when we drink water by small measures,
with astonishment,

the golden city crumbling in the heat,
its battlements dragged down below the palms.
Immovable, a livid mass of lime.

2.

Call this a key,
the lion's paw enflamed, the thorn.
The wicker door is pain, locked,

locked the sea, stripped back,
sheer elongation, corrugated bronze;
the same flesh burning through its gauze.

And will there be no crossing
to rebuild the wall,
eunuchs of Babylon?

For when He claimed creation as His own,
the rind, the flesh, even the blind seed
riding its ark—a voice cried out
You are mistaken, Samael!
O do not lie, Saklas!

3.

As one who stalks forgets to breathe,
listening, peering forward out of time,
emerging—filtered kindlings
under the oaks, a windless pool,

and then a shore, rippled breath
over the shallows, quivering, giraffe-skinned,
till each pebble, sand patch, weed,
untrembles to its place.

That half-life
stirring out of visibility
to swim into the depth
in which all cross-beams disappear:

so gazing, listening,
I too turn to my slow shimmerings.

4.

Unlatched time after time, a fullness
swung and scattered through the ancient woods,
and all that day the source of sound
lay untranslated in the field.

Five-petaled evening opens over us
its amethyst meridian,

a barely lapping filament and stigma
in the open gate.

And I walk farther in the twilight;
a tree-ribbed cave swallows the road
but every surface shines,
cow-parsley, lichen, sand,

even the unignited firefly drifts visibly,
a trailing thread of ash.
All thirsting for the light,
a coral gleam as of unearthly things.

5.

Glints of yeast,
mirrored crumbs of soil,
of gardens moving in the foil,
unending, specular, refused;

leaf, hand, silver knuckle,
and the hollow mouth
whose sound is only glimmering.

6.

Still walking toward it, nearer parts
remaining in their own disguise,
the meadow ghostly in its web.

Night spider, dragon, lion—
what incarnates you, and your high twin
still lingering behind the filamented music insects echo?

—drawing inward to a residue of nothing seen or heard,
original excess, another source
revisiting in fallen sounds, this pallor

draining through the snuffed gleam of each cavity,
the cradle frayed, unmirroring, until there is no frame
though we move through it by a final trial,
unshelled and shadowless.

7.

Midsummer night decipherings,
of joy, still to pass through
and not remain, unhearing,
still to sing of frictions,
winnowings.

Much closer now, a breathlessness away:
wait death, wait there for now;
wait life.

8.

Stirring out of second bondage,
recollected leaf swell, lemon-green
along the willowtails—

was it not *Sophia* rising through the early starlight
like another ring of space,
the milk of other galaxies diffused
above the constellations of mere law?

How even in the dark beyond the orbit
of the sun Her wake resumed the color
of oil beaten to a wider light.

As we once sang across the river
Let our song rise past Him now
Let us return.

9.

So rising from the fire
we let it burn, drawn heavenward
ring after ring, and called it nothing
but the history of another people and their land

though it had been the world.

Autumn

1.

Thoughts of home—a fish-hook
in the soft flesh of the mouth—
and of an earlier world,
the season now midway
between the first flame and the ash.

Seen from above, unnatural
nests of light hang
in the upper branches of a tree,
a webbing of imaginary birds,
the *wisoko* who eats pure fat,
the phoenix rising, steady in the flame—

until I saw it was the river
sliding free beyond the leaves,
the twilight on its back,
soon slipping even that thin bodice
to the serpent of sheer movement easing
beyond time or season past
whatever trash or beauty
gathers along its banks.

How find a patience against that?
The bending tamarisk, almost copper,
the last still shimmer of the cottonwood,
even another moon's slim eyelash,
thin rim of a shard—

too thin for anything but a memento
of the little that remains,
a semblance of the soul
though nothing counterweighs the bodiless
freedom of its passage.

2.

Theseus knew it, half in jest:
the bush, the bear, as if the root
of likeness were sheer terror.

Late-autumn sunlight, warm enough outside
the house, though a cold serpent
creeps between the body and chair.

I look behind me often now
to avoid being startled
by whatever might come near,

knowing some look for God that way,
even those who disbelieve
Him or His coming.

Inside, a cat sleeps on the bed,
a giant red version of it
moving through the air,

the massive jaws returning
for some remnant of the kill—
a scrap, a bleeding mask,

red as the seals of the final days
in which even the smallest ending of a cloud
becomes what it resembles—

labyrinth and Minotaur in one,
fraying edges like old fingers
feeling for the thread.

3.

These are the crumbs of likeness
in a chaos of resemblance,
all things fallen to such small dimensions
they cannot be told apart.

And this is what we eat
after the final days,
this gray-white fluttering of ash,
whose first seed fell like hoarfrost

in the desert, white as coriander seed,
whose taste in that first form
had been like wafers made with honey.
—Who cannot remember,

though we are the last,
and though the Promised Land is this arena
of dry sand that whitens steadily
under the fall of what remains?

4.

Words that weigh nothing—
of fish, of melons, syllables
of garlic and of leeks,
these also we can eat
for they too fall,
they too are of the ash.

I bring you words of the bright
olive and its leaves,
the grape, green as the flesh
of water moving in the sea
when there had been such things.
—These too are finer than the dust.
And though we cannot hold them,
they remain.

5.

Black flames on the white,
inscriptions in the early fires
that we could read.
But that was in the time of harvests,
when the branches bent above the apples,
and the vines were spread apart
with their dark clusters,
and we strung the figs in garlands on the trees;

who even then had thought those flames
were merely ornament, and warnings
were a form of beauty
living in the words themselves.

6.

This too is where the words begin,
in absence and in warning,
blackened characters of sheer withdrawal
burning on the light of what remains.

It is of death, and of recessions,
passages of reference moving
swiftly as the light that turns
upon itself—sheer reaching, objectless—

and all things merely semblances
caught for a moment like these
particles of dust, made visible
as they rise or fall away.

7.

What of the furrows
and the gathering birds,
what of the veil suspended on the loom?

The web has burned away with all its stars,
the cross, the archer, and the swan,
the starry predator and prey;

even the last necessity of law
no different from the blue-white residue
of leaf and fruit after the fire has gone.

Now cold iron clatters on the grate,
as if the stove itself
might be an empty bell,

why does the heart still turn
against that mockery—
why do I say the season was of love?